Easter

Egg

Haunt

This book is fiction. The people, places, events, and bunny gangsters depicted within are fictitious. Any resemblance to persons living or dead or to real life places is purely coincidence and, in all honesty, probably a little disturbing.

ISBN 978-0-9785642-2-3

Printed in the U.S.A.

First Printing, June 2008

Here Comes Patty Rottentail

Stomping Down the Bully Trail

CONTENTS

Real Heroes Read!

realheroesread.com

#5: Easter Egg Haunt

David Anthony
and
Charles David

Illustrations
Lys Blakeslee

Traverse City, MI

Home of the Heroes

abigail

andrew

zoë

CHAPTER 1:
MEET THE HEROES

Welcome to Traverse City, Michigan, population 18,000. The city has everything you might expect: malls, movie theaters, schools, and playgrounds. Kids swim here in the summer and build snowmen during the winter. Sometimes they pretend that they live in an ordinary place.

But Traverse City is far from ordinary. It is set on one of the Great Lakes and blooms with brilliant colors in the spring. Thousands of people visit every year.

Still, few of them know the city's real secret. Even fewer talk about it. You see, Traverse City is home to three exceptional superheroes. This story is about them.

Meet Abigail, the oldest of our heroes by a whole eight minutes. When it comes to sports, she can't be beat—not at equestrian sports, not at the Easter egg-toss, and certainly not at shooting eagles on the golf course. And every year she easily bounces her way to victory in the Annual Bunny-Hop Marathon.

Andrew comes next. He's Abigail's twin brother, younger by a measly eight minutes. If it has wheels, Andrew can ride it. We're talking anything with wheels, no matter the size. From locomotives to tricycles, he is electric, elite, and epic on wheels. He even invented the Super-Spoon Pedal-Painter to make coloring Easter eggs fast and easy.

Last but definitely not least is Baby Zoë. She's proof that big things can come in small packages. She still wears a diaper, but she has x-ray vision that helps her find her Easter basket regardless of where it's hidden. She puts the *extra* in extraordinary.

Together these three heroes keep the streets and neighborhoods of Traverse City and Michigan safe. Together they are …

CHAPTER 2:
ON YOUR MARK

"Excited!" Zoë squealed, barely able to stand still. Not that she was really standing. She was a superhero and could fly. So she was floating in place like a fidgety, excited, baby-sized helicopter.

She and her siblings were waiting for the Read and Seek Egg Hunt to begin behind the Traverse City Public Library. Dozens of other kids crouched to their right and left, all waiting just as impatiently, all thinking the same thing. *Hurry up already!*

Andrew gave Zoë a playful nudge. "Don't you mean *egg*-cited," he smirked.

Zoë and Abigail didn't share their brother's sense of humor. Easter was tomorrow, and they'd had it with Andrew's egg jokes.

"Your brain is scrambled," Abigail groaned.

"Egg-straterrestrial," Zoë said, meaning she thought Andrew was an alien.

The girls, you see, had had it with Andrew's egg jokes because they knew them all. You can't teach an old dog new tricks, they say, and you definitely can't out-yolk—*oops*, out-*joke*—a kid on Easter weekend.

Mrs. Dewey, the director of the library, cleared her throat to get everyone's attention. It worked, too, but the fact that she was wearing a pink bunny costume didn't hurt.

"Remember, children," she said. "The winner of the egg hunt will receive a set of autographed Knightscares books."

A cheer went up through the crowd. Hunting Easter eggs was fun, but autographed books didn't rot and turn your bedroom into a nuclear wasteland if you forgot them under your bed.

"On your mark!" shouted Mrs. Dewey when the crowd quieted.

"Get set!" said Mr. Decimal, the children's librarian. He was also wearing a costume. He was dressed as a giant carrot.

"Hunt!" they cried together, slapping closed the covers of two thick encyclopedias. The noise the books made resembled the firing of a starter's pistol at a track-and-field event.

Bang! GO!

Off they went. Baskets in hand, dozens of kids tore out of the starting gates like wild-eyed Little Red Riding Hoods running from the wolf. Some squealed, some giggled, some even tripped and fell. But all of them had the same goal in mind: Find eggs in two ways—fast and often.

The Read and Seek Egg Hunt was on!

CHAPTER 3:
READ AND SEEK

As you might expect, Abigail, Andrew, and Zoë jumped out to an early lead. Hunting for eggs wasn't much like battling supervillains or saving the world, but don't tell that to the heroes. They knew how to put their powers to work for good and good times.

"Try not to hit *every* bump," Abigail grumped over her shoulder.

"Don't be a back-wagon driver," Andrew retorted.

The two were riding in the typical red wagon. What wasn't typical was that Abigail was fishing off the back end. She cast and caught eggs while Andrew steered.

Meanwhile Zoë took to the air. She was the only one who could, and that gave her an enormous egg-spotting advantage. In fact, she spotted eggs that no one else could possibly see from the ground.

Although there was an important reason for that. No one could spot such eggs from the ground because they were not a part of the Read and Seek Egg Hunt.

Zoë found that out the hard way. Momma and Daddy robin came swooping in to protect their babies. They were Michigan's state bird, and they had recently returned from their winter in Mexico.

"Chirp!" Daddy chirped. "Squawk!" Momma squawked.

"Excuse," Zoë apologized, putting back the eggs and fleeing the nest.

Her mistake, however, affected more than the birds. It slowed her down and gave another egg-hunting team time to catch up.

Rabbit and his sister Princess, two of the heroes' neighbors and friends, were gaining ground. Their baskets brimmed with eggs, and Rabbit's nose was twitching like … well, like a rabbit's in a carrot patch.

His name wasn't really Rabbit, of course, and his sister's wasn't really Princess. But the nicknames fit and so they stuck, and the children didn't mind at all. Princess wanted to be a real princess, and Rabbit liked all things rabbit. That included Easter eggs and the skills to find them.

So the Read and Seek Egg Hunt came down to a competition between two teams. The heroes vs. their neighbors. It was a friendly contest but fierce, and led the participants to search for eggs in unusual and unexpected places.

After her trouble with the birds' nest, Zoë decided to check a safer location. She peeked into Mrs. Dewey's bunny ears with a doctor's otoscope. She figured that rabbit ears were big enough to hide eggs in, and she wouldn't get pecked by angry birds while checking.

Rabbit and Princess investigated every out-of-the-way nook and cranny they could find. They looked in logs, browsed bookshelves, glanced in gutters, and searched the shrubbery. They even called on all their courage and peeked under a porcupine.

Top that, Heroes A²Z. Ouch!

Seeing Rabbit and Princess's determination pushed Abigail to cast and reel faster. She and her siblings couldn't lose or they would never hear the end of it. Three superheroes beaten by just two kids? Talk about having egg on the face! It would be *Easter* egg on her face.

In the end, however, no team won. The game was called on account insane.

Princess, Rabbit, and the heroes stumbled onto something so big that they forgot everything else. Even their Easter baskets slipped from their grips like last year's broken toys.

Something that big should have been impossible, but there it was before their eyes. They couldn't deny what they saw.

CHAPTER 4:
EGG-NORMOUS!

"It's egg-normous!" Andrew gasped, and he wasn't making another lame egg joke this time. He was being totally serious.

The thing standing before him really was an egg. It was also really enormous. It was egg-normous, just like he said. The egg was about the size of a Volkswagen Beetle and was painted for Easter.

Now that was something with wheels that Andrew hadn't ridden … yet.

"You think that's big?" Abigail said. "Imagine the chicken that laid it."

"Edible," Zoë shivered, and Rabbit understood her immediately.

"A chicken that big would look at us like worms," he said. "One peck and we'd be plucked!"

Because none of them wanted to be pecked or plucked, they quickly decided to move the egg. It was the safe and smart thing to do. A giant chicken could show up at any time to claim its property.

Don't doubt it. The heroes had seen stranger things* during their careers as Traverse City's super-heroes.

* See Heroes A2Z #1: Alien Ice Cream

"Zoë, can you carry the egg to the library?" Andrew asked. In the past, he had seen his baby sister carry an iceberg, a giant pie, and a piece of the Mackinac Bridge. Carrying one oversized Easter egg shouldn't be a problem. Of course she could do it.

In fact, she could have carried a whole dozen eggs like this one. It didn't weigh any more than an inflated beach ball.

"Easy," she announced, lifting the giant egg over her head with one hand.

Volleyball, anyone?

Back at the library, Mrs. Dewey and Mr. Decimal took charge. When they saw the egg, their mouths fell open. Then they started to shout instructions.

"Stand back, everyone," Mrs. Dewey said.

"We don't know where that egg has been," added Mr. Decimal.

Those instructions should have been enough, but the pair kept going.

"Don't touch it."

"Be quiet."

"Eat your asparagus."

Sometimes adults just couldn't help being helpful. It was part of their job description.

It took something unexpected to quiet them down. Something that none of them had seen—or *heard*—before.

Thwooo!

From the trees behind the library streaked an orange missile. It whistled in the wind and flew toward the egg like an arrow fired by an Olympic marksman.

Thunk! Crack!

Then it struck and buried itself in the egg. Bullseye! A jagged crack split the egg in several directions, running this way and that like wrinkles in the palm of a person's hand.

As for the missile, even the heroes' mouths fell open when they saw that it was a carrot.

CHAPTER 5:
HAUNTING THE HUNT

"A carrot!" Mrs. Dewey exclaimed. "Who would shoot a carrot at an Easter egg?"

The idea was ridiculous. The day was going from weird to weirder. First the heroes had found a giant painted egg. Now someone was shooting carrots at it.

Had a Valentine's Day cupid given his bow to an angry bunny?

C-R-A-A-A-C-K!

More importantly, what was inside the egg? Because it wasn't done cracking. Whatever was inside the egg would be coming out soon.

"I think it's a baby chicken," Rabbit said.

"Empty?" Zoë guessed, remembering how easy it had been to lift the egg.

Princess shook her head at both of them. "Candy," she said. "Like in a piñata. Everyone knows that princesses deserve more candy."

Unfortunately, their guesses were so wrong that they all would have been booed off a TV game show.

Candy? A chicken? Not even close.

Empty? Forget about it. There was more in that egg than there were bees in a beehive.

And soon they came pouring out. But they weren't bees in the egg. No, they were much worse. A little sting was the last thing the heroes and their friends needed to fear.

Because what came out of the egg was ghosts. Howling, moaning ghosts that were as white as cottage cheese and shaped like the halves of a broken egg. There were dozens and dozens of them. At least one for every person at the Read and Seek Egg Hunt.

Correction. Make that the Read and Seek Egg *Haunt*. Easter had just taken a very spooky turn.

CHAPTER 6:
GULP!

"Run!" Mrs. Dewey shrieked, and the ears on her costume stood up as straight as the hair on the back of her neck. Or was that the *hare* on the back of her neck? She was wearing a rabbit costume after all.

"Run for you lives!" she continued to scream. "The egg is haunted!"

Her warning was completely unnecessary. The crowd knew what was happening. They could see the ghosts. They wanted to run. The problem was, they didn't know where to go.

Ghosts were everywhere—floating, drooling, and chomping their huge mouths. A giant egg, it seemed, could hold a lot of ghosts. And this one had been packed as tight as Mom's suitcase on a three-day weekend.

So no matter where the kids looked to escape, a ghost was waiting. Mrs. Dewey discovered this first. Like every smart librarian, she knew that kids were as important to libraries as books. And while the books were safe, the kids were not.

"Get behind me!" she roared. "Mr. Decimal and I will archive you!"

That was librarian-speak for "keep you safe for twenty or thirty years until someone decides it's time to dust you off and move you to a new safe spot." Which was better than being swallowed.

Yet all her bravery accomplished was getting her and Mr. Decimal swallowed first.

Gulp! A ghost opened wide and Mrs. Dewey went down.

Gulp! Then Mr. Decimal became the second snack.

Just like that, the two of them were captured. They didn't have time to fight back, and they didn't run away. They would never abandon the children. That just wasn't the librarian way—certainly not when readers were in danger!

In fact, no one ran. The rest of the crowd was too stunned by what was happening. They were frozen in fear and shock.

Ghosts were supposed to chase and frighten people. Didn't they watch Scooby-Do? They weren't supposed to swallow librarians whole.

These ghosts weren't normal, and they didn't follow the rules of spook. They were scary, for sure, but they didn't say "Boo!" The only noise they made was a wet smacking of their lips when they swallowed another victim.

Gulp! A little girl wearing an Easter dress disappeared into a ghost's mouth.

Gulp! Even Rabbit was swallowed. All of his bunny know-how couldn't save him from an unpleasant Easter surprise.

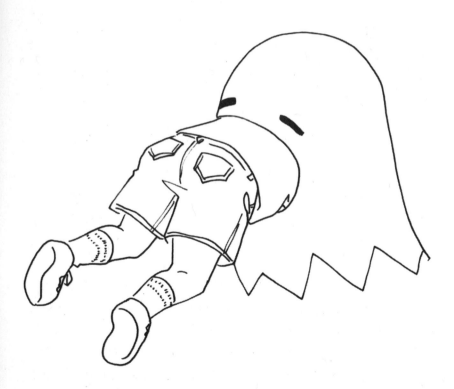

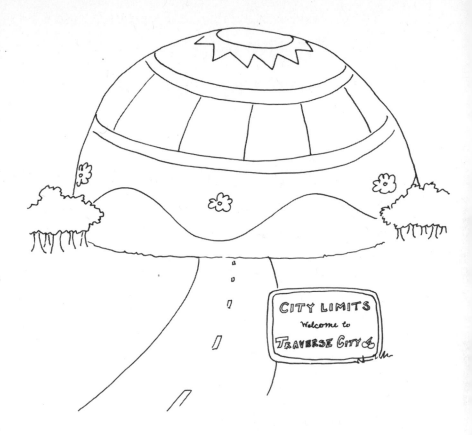

The strangest thing, however, happened next. After gulping down a victim, the ghosts did something even weirder and less ghost-like. They didn't burp or ask to see a dessert menu, and they didn't chase after another human snack. Instead they lay down, closed their eyes, and turned into people-sized Easter eggs. Watching it happen was like watching cement dry in fast-forward.

If the heroes didn't do something soon, all of Traverse City would be trapped inside eggs.

CHAPTER 7:
BREATHING ROOM

Gulp! Gulp!

Ghosts chomped and smacked their lips all over the library grounds. They lurked behind trees. They slinked around corners. Nowhere outside was safe.

Zoë realized that to protect her friends she had to get them indoors.

"Escape!" she cried, waving her arms toward the library like an air traffic controller.

Abigail and Andrew understood her immediately. They wanted to fight the ghosts, of course, but
there were too many of them. There was only one
place to hide. Getting their friends and neighbors to
safety was their first priority.

After that, they would roll up their sleeves and
do what superheroes did best. Kick bad guy butt.

"Put the pedal to the metal," Andrew shouted to his twin.

"Just watch where you're going," she replied. "Keep your eyes on the finish line." Which, in this case, happened to be the library's front doors.

The twins were at it again. Andrew was steering the wagon while Abigail used her athletic power to push. But instead of painted Easter eggs, the wagon was packed with people—as many as could fit plus a few more. Circus clowns in a miniature car had more breathing room.

In fact, to open the doors, they all needed more breathing room. *Breathing* being the keyword. The ghosts were closing in fast, and they couldn't be allowed inside.

"Zoë, use your earthquake blast!" Andrew shouted, remembering the time his sister had knocked over an army of dinosaur skeletons with a single punch*.

"No, your lasers!" Abigail countered, thinking Zoë could zap the ghosts like a space hero from the future.

* See Heroes A2Z #4: Digging For Dinos

But Zoë shook her head and uttered a single word. She had a different plan and it was all about breathing room.

"Exhale," she huffed. Then she sucked in a huge gulp of air and did exactly what she said. She exhaled.

Whoo-oo-oosh!

Straight into the ghosts' surprised faces.

The ghosts fluttered and twirled helplessly like kites caught in a storm. Zoë's super-breath tossed them backward and cleared a path to the library's doors. All she needed was a wig and key and she would have made a perfect modern-day Benjamin Franklin.

"Enter!" she roared, throwing open the library's doors while the ghosts were disoriented. The time to escape was now, not later. In fact, any delay and there would be no later. Everyone would be trapped in ghost eggs.

So in whooshed the wagon with Andrew still at the wheel. Abigail accelerated and Zoë zoomed. Then *boom* went the doors, slamming shut behind them.

The heroes and their friends were safe, but for how long?

CHAPTER 8:
FUNNY BUNNY

Zoë threw her back against the library's doors and spread her arms. Behind her, the ghosts thumped hungrily on the glass and snapped their big mouths open and closed like chewing crocodiles.

"Everybody?" she asked breathlessly, hoping that no one had been left outside.

A quick count told her that everyone had made it into the library. Everyone who could, that is. Mrs. Dewey, Mr. Decimal, Rabbit, and a few others had already been captured. Rescuing them would have to wait.

After that Abigail took charge like the quarter-back in a huddle.

"Andrew, barricade the doors," she said. "Use books, tables, chairs, shelves—anything you can move. Remember, a good defense wins champion-ships."

Next she turned to Princess. "You go long. Check all the windows and make sure they're locked."

Finally she turned to Zoë. "Watch for the blitz," Abigail told her. "If those ghosts break in, I want you to block them. Hold them off to give the others time to run."

Alone in the quiet areas of the library, Princess tiptoed from window to window. So far, so good—they were all locked. At least until she spotted the Easter Bunny.

She blinked. The Easter Bunny! What was he doing outside? He looked so small and afraid. Then she knew. *He must know there are ghosts out there.*

"You poor thing," Princess whispered, unlocking the window and opening it. "You're safe now. Come in."

That was all it took. In an instant, the bunny hopped inside and stuck one of its long feet between the window and the sill. Nothing was closing that window now.

"Wha—?" Princess gasped, but the bunny cut her off.

"Attack!" it screeched in a high-pitched voice. "The library is ours!" Then the ghosts appeared from around a corner and started to pour in through the open window.

In horror, Princess realized that she had done worse than open a can of worms. She had unleashed a pail of poltergeists.

CHAPTER 9:
PATTY ROTTENTAIL

The ghosts swarmed into the library looking for a fight, and Zoë intended to give them one. She met them in the air and with the air from her secret windy weapon. From her lungs and through her lips puffed a second powerful blast.

Whoo-oo-oosh!

But this time the ghosts didn't simply scatter. The library wasn't that large. The ghosts were blown this way and that, but they always bumped into something.

And sooner or later, that something was a some*one*.

Gulp! A ghost bumped into Princess and then swallowed her whole.

Gulp! Gulp! Two more kids disappeared.

"Error!" Zoë wailed, realizing what she had done. Blowing the ghosts away from herself had blown them into other people.

Her shoulders slumped. Her head drooped down. Never had she felt worse or less like a super-hero. She felt so bad, in fact, that she was an easy snack for ghostly attack.

Gulp!

Abigail tried to come to her sister's defense. She dipped into her duffel bag and snatched the first thing she found, which happened to be a football.

As the quarterback, Abigail was expected to handle the ball, but she could do even more. Sports were her specialty. When necessary, she could also *foot* the ball.

"Gulp this!" she snarled at the nearest ghost, and drew back her leg for a punt.

Gulp indeed. That's what happened, all right. First to the football and then to Abigail.

Abigail's foot connected in a mighty kick. The ball went up. The ball went in. Right into a ghost's hungry mouth.

She thought, *It's good!*

So good, in fact, that the ghost wanted more, and Abigail was next on the menu. *Gulp!*

That left Andrew, which was a lot but not nearly enough this time. One hero against dozens of villains was impossible odds, even for the wizard of wheels.

But to his credit, Andrew wouldn't give up. Heroes never did. He leaped onto a cluttered return cart and started rolling and bowling toward the ghosts.

"Time to pay your library fines!" he shouted.

Strike!

Andrew crashed into the ghosts, and his cart somersaulted into the air. Books went flying. Several ghosts were knocked backward and sent spinning.

But it wasn't bowling pins that fell in this strike. It was strike three, Andrew's out. Because the remaining ghosts opened their mouths and closed in on him before he could stand.

Gulp!

In minutes, everyone else in the library had been swallowed and trapped in eggs. With the three heroes out of the way, no one could stand up to the ghosts.

No one but Patty Rottentail, that was. She was the bunny Princess had allowed into the library. She could stand up to the ghosts because she was in charge. The whole Easter Egg Haunt had been her idea.

Grinning wickedly, she flipped open her egg phone and made a quick call.

"The haunting is complete," she said. "Begin Operation Easter Basket."

Then she rubbed her furry little paws together and cackled.

CHAPTER 10:
OPERATION EASTER BASKET

Silence. The library was absolutely still. No voices whispered. No pages rustled. No fingers clacked on keyboards.

While keeping quiet was the library's number one rule, the total silence was eerie. Today it meant defeat, not happy, polite readers. The heroes and their friends had been captured. First they'd been swallowed by ghosts. Then they'd been imprisoned in Easter eggs barely big enough to hold them.

Try as they might, they couldn't break free. There was no way to check out of the library now! Packing a punch while trapped in one of the eggs was impossible.

Not even Zoë could escape. All she could do was squint through the eggshell using her x-ray vision and wait to see what would happen next.

There was no sign of the rabbit mastermind, Patty Rottentail. But a mob of mean-looking bunnies arrived soon. The mob wore striped suits, chewed on toothpicks, and spoke in tough accents. They were also made of chocolate and had bites taken out of their ears. To Zoë, the bunnies looked like old-fashioned gangsters.

"C'mon youse guys," one of them snapped at the others. "Get ta work. Da boss wants us ta load dese eggs onta da truck."

Working in teams of three or four, the bunnies started to carry the eggs outside. There they loaded them onto a flatbed truck that idled in the parking lot.

"Hurry it up dere," a chocolate bunny shouted out the driver's window. "We gotta pretty up da town fast."

Soon all of the eggs were loaded onto the truck, and the driver cranked the vehicle into gear. Slowly it started to chug through the strects of Traverse City.

Not that most people would recognize the town anymore.

Traverse City had changed! Colored streamers dangled from every street sign. Marshmallow chicks peered from windows. Piles of jellybeans poured out of doorways and doghouses. And stringy green Easter grass covered everything like hay in a barn.

Patty Rottentail had called her plan "Operation Easter Basket," and the scheme was easy to figure out. She was turning Traverse City into one giant Easter surprise!

CHAPTER 11:
BREAK A FEW EGGS

Andrew couldn't see what was happening to his friends or to Traverse City. He was trapped in a ghost egg. But he could tell that he and the egg were moving, and knew that couldn't be good.

His mind whirled and wheeled, trying to think of a plan for escape. And that was it—wheels! Wheels could be his plan. If his mind could wheel, the rest of him could, too.

Wheels were his superpower, after all.

So instead of trying to punch and kick his way out of the egg, Andrew started to rock. First left, then right. Then back and forth. He threw his weight from side to side.

In no time the egg responded. It was curved like a wheel and it rolled like one, too—over its fellow eggs, off the edge of the truck, and down onto the street below.

CRACK!

When the egg hit the pavement, Andrew burst free. Once again his wheel skills had saved the day. Who would have guessed that his brain could wheel as well as his feet? Speed and smarts—what a combination!

Still thinking fast, Andrew looped his belt around the truck's trailer hitch and hopped onto a skateboard. Then he let the truck pull him around town like a speedboat towing a water-skier.

Every few blocks, the truck stopped, forcing
Andrew to hide. He would watch from around a corner or bush as the bunnies climbed out of the truck
and unloaded several eggs.

"The eggs are like the star on a Christmas tree,"
Andrew whispered to himself, figuring it out.

It didn't take a rabbit to discover the truth. The
bunnies were placing the eggs at random spots around
town for decoration. They were the final pieces placed
in Patty Rottentail's enormous Easter basket.

Finally Andrew's sisters' eggs were left outside Top of the Ninth, the comic book store on Eighth
Street. What a fitting spot for superheroes! The
chocolate bunnies should have known better, but per-
haps they didn't read.

When the truck disappeared down the street, Andrew went to work. Using a trick he had learned while fighting mutant cherry trees*, he climbed onto his sisters' eggs like a lumberjack onto a log and rolled them into the side of the building.

Double *CRACK!*

In an explosion of shell, Zoë and Abigail were free. First they stretched their limbs and then they flexed their muscles. They were ready and feeling better. It was time to kick some rotten cottontail.

* See Heroes A2Z #3: Cherry Bomb Squad

CHAPTER 12:
PATTY'S PARADE

"Which way did they go?" Abigail asked, standing up and brushing bits of eggshell from her clothing.

"East?" Zoë wondered.

Andrew pointed. "That way," he said. "But they could be anywhere by now. Where would you go if you were a chocolate Easter bunny?"

Andrew's question was a good one, and the right answer could lead the heroes to Patty Rottentail and her chocolate bunny gang. The problem was, the question had more than one possible answer.

"Maybe they went to a craft store," Abigail suggested. "They could find lots of Easter decorations there. Patty Rottentail would feel right at home."

Zoë shook her head. "Eggs," she offered, meaning the heroes should look anyplace eggs could be found.

To Andrew, that meant a grocery store. That was where eggs went no matter where they were laid.

"Let's try Tom's Market," he said, deciding quickly.

Unfortunately the grocery store was a dead end. The heroes didn't find one single egg, bunny, or decoration there. What they were looking for, they discovered, was outside and headed straight for them.

"Did you hear that?" Andrew asked in the parking lot.

"Entertainment," Zoë nodded, cupping an ear with her hand.

A moment later Abigail not only heard it, she saw it.

"Look!" she exclaimed. "It's a parade."

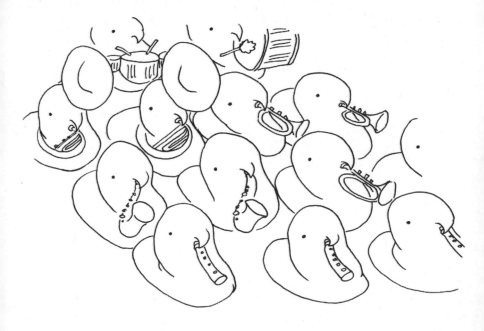

From a distance, the parade looked like any other held on Easter weekend. A marching band stomped in the lead, tooting on brass instruments. Floats followed, towed by tractors. Old-fashioned cars cruised next, bringing up the rear.

First impressions, however, are often deceiving, and this was such a time. Because this marching band wasn't made up of students from a local high school. It was a troop of marshmallow chicks marching in formation like soldiers. And the drivers of the tractors and cars weren't human. They were members of Patty Rottentail's gang.

Even more alarming was the sight of Patty Rottentail herself. She sat high upon a wicker throne that looked like an Easter basket balanced on one end. Below her, a choir of ghosts moaned unfamiliar words to an old familiar song.

Here comes Patty Rottentail
Stompin' down the bully trail.
Stampity, stompity,
Easter's here to stay.

Stickin' every girl and boy
Into an egg like Easter toys.
Stuckity, stickity,
They'll be stuck that way.

"Earsplitting," Zoë winced as the parade approached, and her siblings readily agreed.

Patty Rottentail's song was painful to hear. The words were wrong. The singers sang in strange voices. The whole parade sounded and looked more like a conqueror's victory march than a celebration.

Worst of all, Patty Rottentail was surrounded and well guarded. To get to her, the heroes would have to fight an army.

Had Abigail, Andrew, and Zoë finally met their match?

CHAPTER 13:
CHOCOLATE AMBUSH

Still covering their ears, the heroes hid until the parade passed. Not even they could challenge an entire army by themselves. The heroes had to pick their spots more carefully than that. All of Traverse City was counting on them.

When the parade finally rounded a corner and disappeared, Abigail let out a growl.

"The clock is running out," she said. "It's time for our two-minute drill."

She meant that the heroes had to hurry, like a football team trying to come back and win at the end of the game. Patty Rottentail had already turned most of Traverse City into a giant Easter basket. She could strike anywhere next, anytime.

Naturally the best way to hurry was for Andrew to use his superpower.

"Everybody in," he said, coasting over to his sisters on the back of a shopping cart borrowed from the grocery store.

Abigail and Zoë glanced at the cart and then at each other. They trusted Andrew, of course. They had seen his wheeled wizardry in action enough times. But they also wondered why he found such weird contraptions to ride so often. Freezers, baby buggies, lawn mowers, and now a shopping cart. There was nothing wrong with an average, everyday bicycle!

Or maybe there was something about bicycles that Andrew didn't like. Because in very little time, he had himself and his sisters speeding down the street. Few bicycles had ever traveled so fast.

Soon the parade came back into view and Andrew put on the brakes. He wanted to follow Patty Rottentail and her gang, not pass them in a race.

"They're headed for the mall," he said. "We can sneak in by the movie theater."

Inside the mall was as quiet as a ghost town. No shoppers strolled the long corridors. No teenagers loitered in the food court. Except for the fresh Easter paint on the walls, the place could have been abandoned years ago.

"Eerie," Zoë whispered, thinking of Patty Rottentail's ghosts. Today the mall seemed like the perfect place to haunt, and she knew they weren't alone.

She was only half right. The heroes weren't alone in the mall, but it wasn't ghosts they had to worry about. Not at the moment anyway.

Now it was time for the chocolate bunnies to hop into action. And hop they did—*boing, boing, boing!*—from behind counters, clothing racks, bookshelves, and doors.

"Get 'em!" shouted their leader, raising a chocolate tommy-gun and taking aim.

CHAPTER 14:
RAT-A-TAT-TAT!

Suddenly *rat-a-tat-tat* and *bang, bang, bang* filled the air. The bunny gangsters fired shots from everywhere. But instead of bullets, their chocolate tommy-guns fired baby carrots at the heroes.

"It's an ambush!" Andrew cried.

"Scramble!" Abigail yelped.

For several minutes, the heroes used their powers to elude the bunny blitz. Like a wheel Andrew rolled, somersaulting and cartwheeling out of the way. Abigail whirled and spun on light fixtures and an Easter banner hanging overhead like a gold medal-winning gymnast. Zoë zipped from side to side in the air with blinding speed.

Their acrobatic skills, however, couldn't keep them safe forever. The bunnies were firing too many carrots, and even heroes get tired eventually.

Thwack! A lucky shot finally struck Andrew's hip and sent him spinning to his knees. He raised his arms, but more shots immediately followed. All of them pierced his sleeves or pant legs. In no time he was pinned to the floor.

After that, the bunnies concentrated on Abigail and Zoë. Two targets were easier to track than three.

Thwack! Thwack!

Zoë went down next, if going down could mean getting pinned to the ceiling. Shots riddled her cape, and she was hung out to dry like laundry on a clothesline.

Abigail stubbornly continued to flip and twirl, knowing that it was only a matter of time before she, too, was pinned. Her superhero's heart just wouldn't let her give up.

Rat-a-tat-tat! Carrots blazed to her left and right. *Bang, bang, bang!* They whisked past her ears.

Still she thought for a moment that she could reach her brother. One triple-back salto dismount should do it.

Thwack! Thwack! Thwack!

Too slow! She spun, the carrots struck, and she was pinned to the wall like a Green Day poster.

"Hold your fire!" the boss bunny ordered his troops. "It's over. We got 'em."

He was confident and smiling and proud of himself. He and his gang had defeated Traverse City's superheroes. No one would ever take another bite out of their ears.

The big boss, Patty Rottentail, would reward him for that. Maybe he would get to ride on the float with her in the next parade. Maybe the ghosts would even sing a song about him.

Such selfish dreams! They were not meant to be. Because this bunny was about to learn the meaning of the expression, "Don't count your chickens before they're hatched."

Especially when the chickens were really superhero kids who knew how to scramble rotten eggs.

CHAPTER 15:
HEROES IN DISGUISE

Superheroes come in all shapes, sizes, ages, and abilities. Some are average teenagers who go to school and complain about homework. Others are massively muscled adults with regular jobs by day and crime-fighting duties at night.

What most of them have in common, however, is a costume. They wear one to protect their real identities, to let people know who they are, or just to look cool.

Even Abigail, Andrew, and Zoë wore costumes. They didn't usually show them off, but they always wore them under their clothes in case of emergencies.

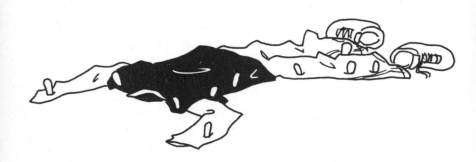

And right now was just such an emergency. The heroes were trapped. They were pinned to the floor, ceiling, and wall by carrots through their clothing. Their clothes were literally holding them back.

So they made like Superman in a telephone booth. Off came their clothes and out came their costumes. In no time the heroes were free and their powers unleashed.

In a flash, Abigail became

TRIPLE A, THE ALL-AMERICAN ATHLETE.

Her red, white, and blue colors never ran, and
neither did she.

Maybe you've heard of Kid Rock. Well, in his costume, Andrew became

KID ROLL.

He always rocked at 100 mph, and his roll left the competition far behind.

Only Zoë didn't change much. Nothing but her shirt. An extra capital letter *Z* on her chest transformed her from regular Zoë into

ZUPER ZOË.

Bunny baddies beware!

Zuper Zoë shook a finger at the chocolate bunnies like an owner scolding a pet. Tsk, tsk, tsk. "Educate," she told them. It was time for her and her siblings to teach the bunny gangsters a lesson.

CHAPTER 16:
TRAPPED AGAIN

The lesson the heroes taught the chocolate bunnies was simple and short. Everyone earned an A+ whether they wanted to or not.

Andrew began the instruction by luring several bunnies onto the mall's carousel. Not many malls had a carousel, but the Grand Traverse Mall did. It was one more reason why Traverse City was a great place.

For everyone but gangster bunnies, that is. Andrew got them spinning so fast that they passed out and never got up. They turned back into regular chocolate treats from then on. The kind you could bite that didn't bite back.

Jackrabbit Sports

At least a dozen other bunnies chased Abigail into a sporting goods store. It wasn't their smartest move. It was like following Batman into the Bat-cave. All of his secret gadgets were there.

First there came a *bang* and a *crash*, and then things got really loud. *Ka-boom!* Balls, clubs, sneakers, and skates hurtled through the air. The bunnies didn't know what hit them again and again and again. *Pow!*

"Fore!" Abigail shouted just before the noise faded. Then everything in the sporting goods store was quiet except for the little birdies that the bunnies thought they heard.

After that, the only other noise in the mall came from the food court.

Burrrrrp!

Or more specifically, from Zoë in the food court.

Andrew and Abigail found her sitting alone at a table with chocolate smeared all over her lips and chin. She clutched a half-empty jar of creamy peanut butter in one hand and a tall glass of chocolate milk in the other. Then was no sign of the chocolate bunnies anywhere.

"What happened to the gangsters?" Abigail asked.

Zoë grinned, showing chocolate-stained teeth.

"Eaten," she burped, leaving no doubt. Chocolate bunnies were delicious.

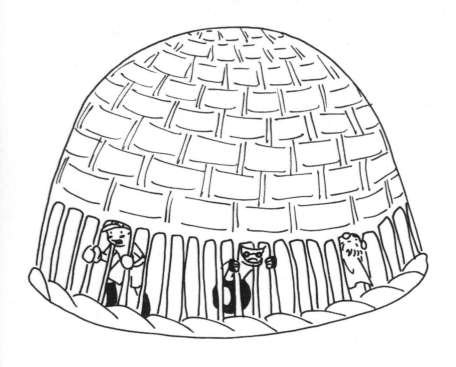

The heroes were about ready to congratulate themselves when they heard a loud noise overhead. *Snick!* Something mechanical was moving.

They looked up in time to see a huge upside-down Easter basket fall from the ceiling.

"It's a trap!" Andrew howled.

"Eek!" Zoë cried.

They were too late. The enormous basket fell on them like a net on a butterfly. They were trapped again.

CHAPTER 17: CARROT FU

The next sound heard in the mall's food court was laughter. High-pitched, squeaky, insane bunny laughter.

"I win!" Patty Rottentail cackled. "I win, I win, I win! Easter is mine!"

The bunny hopped from behind a pizza counter, laughing and holding her belly in her paws. The look in her eyes was wild.

"So much for Traverse City's heroes," she sneered. "Look at you. You're caged like pet rabbits. I win!"

"Don't be so sure," Abigail replied. "We've made bigger comebacks before. Show her, Zoë!"

Zoë nodded and sprang into action. She was happy to be doing something besides listening to Patty Rottentail laugh. The bunny's annoying voice reminded her of cats fighting.

"Elevate!" Zoë shouted, flying straight up with her hands above her head. When her palms slapped against the upside-down Easter basket, she lifted it into the air. Then she threw it across the food court. *Crash!*

Frightened for possibly the first time, Patty Rottentail started to think fast. The heroes had escaped yet another of her traps, and she was running out of surprises. To win, she needed to divide and conquer. Three heroes were too many to face at once.

"Have a nice trip!" she screeched at Abigail and Andrew. "See you next fall." Then she tossed two heaping handfuls of jellybeans onto the floor at the heroes' feet.

Abigail hit them immediately and started to slip. Her arms and legs whirled crazily for balance.

Luckily Andrew caught his sister before she fell. The jellybeans were like tiny wheels to him. No trouble at all. In fact, he could walk safely over jellybeans, marbles, gumballs, and even misplaced skateboards.

Still, the jellybeans slowed him and his sister down. Which was what Patty Rottentail wanted. Divide and conquer. Now the bunny could face Zoë alone.

Alone with her secret weapon.

"Eee-yah!" Patty Rottentail shrieked, whipping out her carrot-handled nunchuku. Like the star of an old kung fu movie, she whirled the weapon over her shoulders, around her waist, and between her legs. She was definitely a master of Carrot Fu. Even her belt was orange.

Undaunted, Zoë sped down to meet the bunny nose-to-nose, or nose-to-whisker as the case may be. This was it, the final battle. The winner here would win the war.

"Eee—!" Zoë started to cry.

"—yah!" Patty Rottentail finished.

Their battle was underway.

The bunny attacked first, swinging her nunchuku like a sword. Zoë countered with her hands and feet, smoothly blocking Patty's swipes. Zoë knew some martial arts tricks herself. She was a black belt in Tae Kwon Diaper.

    Their fight could have gone on forever. The two were quite easily matched. Swing, block! Chop, clock! Neither could gain an advantage.

    Not until Zoë used her mind as well as her muscles. Every hero knew it took both to win.

    Patty's nunchuku slashed close to Zoë's face. But instead of ducking, Zoë opened her mouth wide and bit. *Chomp!* She caught one end of the nunchuku in her teeth like a dog snatching a Frisbee out of mid-air.

"Edible," Zoë grunted between her clenched teeth. Nothing would make her let go of the nunchuku.

Patty Rottentail realized this immediately. While Zoë hadn't won, she had thought up a way to keep herself from losing. No weapon, no victory for Patty.

So the bunny did what bullies do when things get tough. She gave up and ran. But not before calling on her ghosts for help.

"Stop them!" she squealed. "Give me time to escape!"

Quickly the ghosts floated out from their hiding places around the mall. Even more quickly they completely surrounded the heroes.

CHAPTER 18:
PICTURE PERFECT

The heroes eyed the ghosts. The ghosts eyed them. It was like an old-fashioned staring contest, and neither side wanted to blink first.

But someone finally did, and that someone was Andrew. He blinked when Zoë scooped him up and threw him over the ghosts.

He screamed, too, and loud. "What's the big idea?"

Crash!

Andrew landed in a crowd of mannequins that were standing just inside a clothing store. His arms got tangled in their arms. His legs mixed up with theirs. When he finally pushed and shoved his way to freedom, he came up wearing an outfit fit for a king.

The King of Clowns, that is. Imagine an explosion in a Halloween costume shop. Andrew looked like the leftovers.

Clown or not, he wasn't laughing. Neither were the ghosts. They saw that he had escaped and started rapidly floating toward him.

"Entrap!" Zoë shouted, hoping her brother would catch on. She had thrown him into the mannequins for a reason.

And catch on he did, just in time. When the first ghost glided near, Andrew heaved a mannequin straight at its face. *Gulp!* The ghost swallowed the mannequin whole. Then, just as Zoë had hoped, the ghost turned into an Easter egg.

"You're a genius, Zoë!" Andrew exclaimed.

"Enlightened," she agreed with a wink. Her plan was perfect. Forcing the ghosts to eat turned them into harmless eggs.

In little time, Andrew fed the remaining ghosts their final meal. It was mannequins for breakfast, mannequins for lunch, and mannequins for dinner. No one needed a second helping.

The heroes were about to celebrate their victory when a loud noise interrupted them.

Vroom! Vroo-oommm!

They spun to see Patty Rottentail sitting in a long hot rod shaped like a carrot. The bunny revved the engine to get their attention.

"See you next time, zeroes," she snarled. "Easter comes every year."

Then she punched the gas pedal and the tires squealed. In a cloud of smoke, she and her hot rod disappeared.

She wasn't gone for good, the heroes knew. Patty Rottentail would return. But this Easter had been saved, and Traverse City was safe again.

All that was left to do now was to break a few eggs. A few hundred dozen actually. Patty Rottentail's ghosts had gobbled up almost everyone in town.

Everyone including the real Easter Bunny. The heroes found him in a ghost egg back at the library. He was so happy at being rescued that he posed for pictures with everyone from the Read and Seek Egg Hunt. Then he bounded off to work. The day before Easter was, understandably, his busiest time.

Even the heroes slowed down long enough to have their picture taken. But like the Easter Bunny, they couldn't sit still for long. Protecting Traverse City and the rest of Michigan was a full-time job. Danger could arise in the most unlikely places, even in …

Book #6:
Fowl Mouthwash

Visit the Website

realheroesread.com

Meet Authors Charlie & David
Read Sample Chapters
See Fan Artwork
Join the Free Fan Club
Invite Charlie & David to Your School
Lots More!

Fighting Crime Before Bedtime

... and more!

Also by David Anthony and Charles David

Monsters. Magic. Mystery.

#1: Cauldron Cooker's Night
#2: Skull in the Birdcage
#3: Early Winter's Orb
#4: Voyage to Silvermight
#5: Trek Through Tangleroot
#6: Hunt for Hollowdeep
#7: The Ninespire Experiment
#8: Aware of the Wolf

Visit
www.realheroesread.com
to learn more

#1: Cauldron Cooker's Night

#2: Skull in the Birdcage

#3: Early Winter's Orb

#4: Voyage to Silvermight
The Dragonsbane Horn Book One

#5: Trek Through Tanglewood
The Dragonsbane Horn Book Two

#6: Hunt the Gallowgeck
The Dragonsbane Horn Book Three

#7: The Vinespire Experiment

#8: Aware of the Wolf

ABIGAIL

TRIPLE A
ALL AMERICAN ATHLETE

ANDREW

KID ROLL

BABY ZOË

ZUPER ZOË

Connect with the Authors

Charlie:
charlie@realheroesread.com
facebook.com/charlesdavidclasman

David:
david@realheroesread.com
facebook.com/authordavidanthony

realheroesread.com

facebook.com/realheroesread
youtube.com/user/realheroesread
twitter.com/realheroesread
twitter.com/charliedclasman

Sigil Publishing, LLC

www.sigilpublishing.com

P.O. Box 824
Leland, MI 49654

Email:
info@sigilpublishing.com

Want to Order Your Very Own Autographed
Heroes A2Z or Knightscares Book?

Here's How:

(1) Check the books you want on the next page.
(2) Fill out the address information at the bottom.
(3) Add up the total price for the books you want.

Heroes A²Z cost $4.99 each.

(4) Add $1.00 shipping per book.
(5) Michigan residents include 6% sales tax.
(6) Send check or money order along with the next page to:

Real Heroes Read!
P.O. Box 654
Union Lake, MI 48387

Thank You!

Please allow 3-4 weeks for shipping

Total $ Enclosed: _____

Autograph To: _____

Name: _____

Address: _____

City, State, Zip: _____

About the Illustrator
Lys Blakeslee

Lys graduated from Grand Valley State University in Michigan where she pursued a degree in Illustration.

She has always loved to read, and devoted much of her childhood to devouring piles of books from the library.

She lives in Wyoming, MI with her wonderful parents, two goofy cats, and one extra-loud parakeet.

Thank you, Lys!